PUFFIN BOOKS

Stardust
STOLEN MAGIC

Linda Chapman lives in Leicestershire with her
family and two Bernese mountain dogs. When
she is not writing she spends her time looking
after her two young daughters, horse riding and
teaching drama.

Stardust
STOLEN MAGIC

Linda Chapman

Illustrated by Angie Thompson

PUFFIN

To Iola and Amany –

my precious stardust spirits

PUFFIN BOOKS

Published by the Penguin Group
Penguin Books Ltd, 80 Strand, London WC2R 0RL, England
Penguin Group (USA) Inc., 375 Hudson Street, New York, New York 10014, USA
Penguin Group (Canada), 90 Eglinton Avenue East, Suite 700, Toronto, Ontario, Canada M4P 2Y3
(a division of Pearson Penguin Canada Inc.)
Penguin Ireland, 25 St Stephen's Green, Dublin 2, Ireland
(a division of Penguin Books Ltd)
Penguin Group (Australia), 250 Camberwell Road,
Camberwell, Victoria 3124, Australia (a division of Pearson Australia Group Pty Ltd)
Penguin Books India Pvt Ltd, 11 Community Centre,
Panchsheel Park, New Delhi – 110 017, India
Penguin Group (NZ), 67 Apollo Drive, Rosedale, North Shore 0632, New Zealand
(a division of Pearson New Zealand Ltd)
Penguin Books (South Africa) (Pty) Ltd, 24 Sturdee Avenue,
Rosebank, Johannesburg 2196, South Africa

Penguin Books Ltd, Registered Offices: 80 Strand, London WC2R 0RL, England

penguin.com

First published 2006
4
This edition published 2007 for Index Books Ltd

Text copyright © Linda Chapman, 2006
Illustrations copyright © Angie Thompson, 2006
All rights reserved

The moral right of the author and illustrator has been asserted

Set in Monotype Bembo

Made and printed in England by Clays Ltd, St Ives plc

ISBN-13: 978-0-14131-782-3
ISBN-10: 0-141-31782-5

One

A full moon shone in the sky, its silver rays lighting up the fallen leaves in the clearing below. Leaping down from an oak tree, a grey squirrel scampered across the grass. It stopped suddenly, its dark eyes flicking upwards as three girls came swooping through the sky, laughing and shouting.

'Got you!' Lucy Evans gasped, her

fingertips grabbing Faye's blue dress.
Her long, chestnut-brown hair swirled
around her as she reached for Ella. 'Got
you both!' she said as Ella squealed and
ducked away too late.

Lucy hovered in the air, her own dress glittering golden in the starlight. 'Where's Allegra?' she demanded.

The air behind her quivered slightly as her best friend, Allegra Greenwood, appeared in mid-air right behind her. 'Here I am!'

'Cheat!' Ella protested. 'We didn't say we could camouflage ourselves, Allegra.'

Allegra tossed back her blonde curls. 'We didn't say we couldn't.'

Seeing her chance, Lucy dived for Allegra. 'Tick!' she exclaimed, touching Allegra's silver dress.

Allegra laughed. 'All right. You got me. Who's on next?'

'We should get on with the work we've got to do,' Faye said, flying down to the ground. 'This clearing's going to take a bit of sorting out to get it ready for winter.'

Lucy joined her. The trees' branches were half-bare and the ground was thick with leaves. When she had first found out that she was a stardust spirit, the leaves had been new and birds had been nesting in the branches. It was hard to believe that just seven months ago, she had never heard of stardust spirits. It had been Allegra who had told her all about them. She had explained to her that every human has stardust inside them but that some special people have more stardust than others. These people, Allegra had told Lucy, have the ability to turn into stardust spirits at night-time – but only if they believe in magic enough.

Lucy had discovered that she was a stardust spirit and now, every night, she flew to meet the other stardust spirits in the woods. Once there, she helped the other spirits look after the natural world, caring for plants and animals and repairing any damage done to nature by thoughtless humans. To help them in their work, they had magic powers.

The squirrel scampered towards Lucy. She crouched down. 'Hello, little one,' she said softly.

He stopped beside her, his bright eyes curious but unafraid.

Lucy smiled. One of the best things about being a stardust spirit was being able to get close to the wild animals that lived in the woods. Some powerful spirits could even talk to animals. Lucy longed to be that powerful. *Maybe one day*, she thought, glancing up at the stars.

Power seemed to glow and glitter across the night sky. Lucy straightened up, excitement fizzing through her at the thought of doing magic.

'Come on, you guys,' she called to

Allegra and Ella, who were still arguing about whether camouflaging, another type of stardust magic that made the spirit appear to vanish into the background, was allowed when you were playing tick. 'Faye's right – we should get started on this clearing.'

'So what shall we do first?' Faye asked, as Ella and Allegra flew down. She was the smallest of the four girls and looked like a pixie with her short blonde hair and heart-shaped face. 'Should we get rid of the leaves?'

'Not all of them,' Allegra replied. 'Having leaves on the ground protects spring plants like snowdrops and bluebells from frost and it's good cover for small animals.' Allegra knew more about the woods than any of them. Her mum, Xanthe, was a stardust spirit too. 'We need to get rid of the leaves that are clogging up the bushes so it makes it easier for animals to make homes to hibernate in, and then we need to make sure that the trees are healthy, with no broken branches or diseased patches, and that they have enough water near their roots.'

'Well, if you blow the leaves into piles, Allegra,' Faye suggested, 'I can water the trees using my magic.' Allegra was an autumn spirit, which meant she could conjure wind. Faye was a winter spirit, which gave her the power to control water; she could make it rain or hail or snow.

There were four types of stardust spirit in all – spring, summer, autumn and winter – and each had their own powers.

Ella, who was a spring spirit and could make things grow, said, 'I'll grow some more brambles to provide places that hedgehogs and rabbits and other animals can hibernate in.'

Lucy frowned, thinking about what she could do. Being a summer spirit, she could heat things up and start fires, but how would that help? 'I suppose I could burn the diseased trees down,' she suggested. 'I could use fire to get rid of the broken branches.'

'Great!' Allegra exclaimed. 'Let's get started.'

The girls set to work. Lucy walked over to where there was an alder tree with a large half-broken branch.

Lucy raised her hands. 'Fire be with me!' she whispered, pointing at the branch. Heat flooded down her arm. There was a crackle and suddenly the branch was alight.

Yes! Lucy thought excitedly. The branch blazed, the fire eating up the dead wood. As the flames began to flick up the trunk to the healthy part of the tree, Lucy pointed her hands again and the fire went no further.

There was a creak and the burnt branch fell off. It fell into the dry leaves and flames sparked upwards. 'Fire be gone!' Lucy commanded.

With a hiss the flames extinguished.

Feeling power buzzing through her, Lucy grinned. When she had first become a stardust spirit she had found it hard to control her magic, but now it was easy. She turned to the next tree – an old oak tree in the middle of a huddle of other trees. Its trunk was split in two and its bark was dark with disease. That would be her next target. But, she realized, a few trees along from it there was another diseased tree, and then there was another tree with a heavy branch that was broken. There were so many that needed sorting out. It was going to take ages, unless . . .

An idea flashed into her mind.

Could I do it? she wondered, her heart quickening. *It would be much faster.*

She took a deep breath and looked at the cluster of trees. In her mind she pictured a lion made out of stars – the constellation of Leo, the constellation that contained the Royal Star of Regulus that gave all summer spirits their power. It was too early in the night for Leo to be visible in the night sky but as she imagined all the stars that formed his shape, Lucy felt magic spark through her.

'Shield be with me!' she whispered, pointing at the trees surrounding the oak. Magic tingled over her skin. The air around the trees seemed to tremble. Concentrating hard, Lucy felt power flooding into her from the stars.

'Fire be with me!' Her words rang out – powerful and strong – almost not sounding like her voice at all.

For a second, Lucy registered that Allegra, Faye and Ella had swung

round to look at her but then there was a great whooshing noise and her attention snapped to the cluster of trees. The diseased trees burst into fire, flames shooting up into the sky in a column of intense heat.

Lucy vaguely heard her friends' shocked gasps, but power was beating through her, stronger and more forceful than anything she had ever known, and she lost herself in the feeling. This was real magic! Caught in the moment, she felt as if she could see every bump on every twig, every vein on every leaf of the trees caught in the fire.

More, she thought, welcoming the power. *I want more.*

'Lucy!' Faye's alarmed cry filtered

into Lucy's mind. 'Rain,' Faye gasped, pale with fright, 'be with . . .'

'Fire be gone!' Lucy's forceful command cut across her words.

There was a crackle and the fire vanished, leaving a cloud of smoke and ash. Lucy breathed out a long and trembling sigh as she felt the power draining away. The next second, she was surrounded by her friends.

'What happened there? I thought the whole clearing was going to go up in flames.' Allegra coughed as she breathed in the smoke. 'Wind be with me!' she commanded, instantly conjuring up a breeze to blow away the smoke.

'Oh, Lucy!' exclaimed Faye. 'Did you lose control? I thought I was going to have to try and put it all out with some rain.'

'We're going to have to re-grow all the trees and bushes near that oak now,' said Ella, looking dismayed.

A smile spread across Lucy's face. A delicious feeling of triumph was coursing through her. 'No, we're not.'

The others frowned.

'Look,' Lucy told them.

They swung round to where the trees had been. The diseased and damaged trees and wood had gone but not a single leaf of any of the healthy trees had been burnt or harmed in any way. The only reminder of the fire was a pile of smouldering ashes and the last few wisps of smoke that Allegra's breeze was blowing across the clearing.

'There's no damage to the good trees,' Ella said slowly.

'No,' Lucy replied. Excitement coursed through her. *I did it! I did it!* The words rang like a bell in her head. She'd burnt all the bad wood but kept all the good.

'But how . . .?' Faye began wonderingly.

'I know!' Allegra's eyes widened. 'You used your higher powers, didn't you, Lucy? You used them at the same time as your normal summer magic?'

Lucy nodded. As well as their normal powers, all stardust spirits also had higher powers, which were much harder to use and control. As a summer spirit Lucy could cast a magical shield around anything she wished to protect.

And that was what she had done to the healthy trees. She had never tried using her shield magic and her fire magic at the same time, but it had been an awesome feeling.

Faye's hand flew to her mouth.

'Wow!' Allegra said, looking at Lucy with sudden respect.

'Lucy!' Ella said sounding more horrified than impressed.

'What?' Lucy said. She'd expected some sort of reaction but her friends were looking at her as if she was some sort of alien. 'What's the matter?'

'Didn't you know that you're not supposed to do both types of magic at once?' Ella demanded. 'That it's dangerous?'

'I was told we shouldn't try it until we were much older,' Faye agreed.

'I didn't know,' Lucy said, feeling uncomfortable.

Allegra grinned at her. 'Well, I think it was cool, Luce. I've never heard of anyone our age doing both types of magic at once. It's amazing you managed it.'

Lucy shot her a grateful smile.

'Do it again,' Allegra went on. 'It'll get the clearing sorted out much quicker.'

'No,' Ella protested. 'It might be dangerous!'

Lucy hesitated. She longed to do her magic again, but seeing Ella's face she knew that if she did, it would just cause an argument. 'Don't worry, Ella,' she sighed. 'I'll just use my fire magic.'

They got back to work. Lucy carefully burnt just one tree at a time until the only trees left were healthy trees with strong branches, but all the time she kept remembering what it had felt like to have so much power flooding through her from the stars. She didn't care if it was dangerous. She *had* to do it again.

'That magic you did back in the clearing was awesome,' Allegra said as she and Lucy swooped across the fields on their way home later that night.

Lucy secretly agreed but she didn't want her best friend accusing her of getting big-headed, so she just shrugged as if it was no big deal. 'Thanks.' She quickly changed the subject. 'So did you see that removals van outside Lavender Cottage this afternoon?' she asked.

Allegra lived in Willow Cottage to the left of Lucy's house, Jasmine Cottage. Lavender Cottage was on the other side.

Allegra nodded. 'The new people must be moving in. I wonder what they're like.'

'Maybe we'll meet them in the morning,' Lucy said. 'What time are you coming round?'

Allegra was coming to stay for the weekend while her mum, Xanthe, was away at a natural medicine conference.

'About nine if that's OK,' Allegra

replied. 'Xanthe needs to leave then.'

At first Lucy had found it hard to get used to Allegra calling Xanthe by her first name instead of calling her Mum, but now she was used to it. Sometimes it seemed that Xanthe was more like Allegra's friend or big sister than her parent. She was young for a mum and she didn't seem to set many rules for Allegra. Not like Lucy's parents, who were very strict.

'OK, I'll see you then,' Lucy said as they reached their cottages. 'Night!'

Swooping in through her bedroom window, she landed in her room. Usually she said the words that changed her back straight away, in case anyone came in, but now she didn't. She went to the window and stared

out at the stars. The constellation of
Leo was now rising in the skies.

In her mind she traced the pattern of
the stars – head, mane, chest, legs –
until she could see the shape of a lion.

Leo, Lucy thought. She had looked
up the constellation of Leo on the
Internet and found that it was supposed
to represent a legendary lion who had
been very strong. The warrior Hercules
had fought the lion and eventually
won. Afterwards he had worn the lion's
skin as a cloak and it had kept him safe
from harm. That was why summer
spirits had the power to conjure up
magical shields of protection. The
higher powers all stardust spirits had
were linked to the myths that
surrounded their constellations.

Leo seemed to draw Lucy into its brightness. She remembered the feeling when she'd used both her fire and shield magic together. She longed to feel that power again. But she knew that Ella and probably Faye would stop her. Unless she wasn't with them; unless she was on her own . . .

I could go back now.

The second the thought flashed across her mind, she wanted to do it.

I won't be long, she thought impulsively. *And it's not like anything will go wrong.*

Before she could change her mind, she dived out through the window and flew into the dark night.

CHAPTER

Two

Lucy swooped down into a clearing of oak and beech trees. As she landed on the short autumn grass, a breeze ruffled her hair. She looked around. It was strange being on her own in the woods. She was nearly always with the others. That was the way the stardust world worked – you were supposed to work with other spirits.

So what am I doing now?

Lucy pushed the thought away. She just wanted to try using her magic, that was all.

Identifying a healthy oak tree with several branches of dead wood, she looked at the sky and began to trace the shape of Leo. Her arms began to tingle. 'Shield be with me!' She pointed her left hand at the healthy parts of the tree. 'Fire be with me!' She pointed her right hand at the dead branches.

Magic flowed into her from the stars. The dead branches burst into flames.

More, Lucy thought, pulling power down from the skies. *I want more!*

But as the thought was crossing her brain she saw the fire reaching high into the sky and alarm flashed through her. 'Fire be gone!' she commanded.

At once the fire dropped. The air in the clearing was thick with grey smoke and, staggering slightly as the power drained out of her, Lucy began to cough. Tears smarted in her eyes and she found herself wishing she had Allegra's power to conjure a wind to blow the smoke away.

Backing away to the far side of the clearing, she rubbed her smarting eyes. As she did so, she had the strange feeling that someone was watching her. She swung round. Who was it?

Her eyes caught sight of a black cat in the bushes. Lucy sighed with relief. 'Hey there, puss. You gave me a fright.'

The cat stared at her with unblinking green eyes.

Lucy went a few steps nearer and held out her hand. 'Hello.'

The cat hissed and spat. Lucy jerked back in surprise. Turning round with a yowl, the cat raced away into the night.

Lucy stared after it, her heart thumping. She'd never known an animal run away from her before. Animals always liked her. Even the most shy of them would come and be petted by her.

It's no big deal, she told herself. *It was just a cat running off.* But she felt slightly spooked. She turned back to the clearing and started in surprise. A figure in a long silver dress was flying towards her through the trees.

'Xanthe!' Lucy exclaimed, all thoughts of the weird cat going straight out of her head at the sight of Allegra's mum.

'Lucy!' Xanthe looked equally surprised. She landed on the short grass. 'I saw the smoke above the trees and thought there might be a fire or some trouble. What are you doing here? Where are the others?' She looked around.

Lucy felt awkward. 'They've gone home. We all did but I came back because . . .' She hesitated. She had a feeling that telling Xanthe she had come back to work powerful magic on her own would *not* be a good plan. 'Because I left my star stone anklet here earlier,' she lied, pointing to the chain around her ankle with its black and white onyx stone.

'I see.' Xanthe's eyes flicked to where the cat had been and she frowned as if trying to figure something out. But then she shook her head and looked back at Lucy. 'So where did all the smoke come from?'

'Um . . . well, when I was here I saw a few trees that looked diseased and I decided to burn them down,' Lucy admitted.

'On your own?' Xanthe questioned.

'Yes,' Lucy replied, feeling uncomfortable.

Xanthe's eyes bored into her. Lucy looked down at the ground. She could feel herself blushing.

'Well,' Xanthe said slowly, 'it seems

you've found your anklet now, so you might as well be getting home.'

'Yes,' Lucy said in relief. 'I'll go now.'

Xanthe nodded. 'And, Lucy,' she said as Lucy turned to take off. 'For the future, doing magic on your own is not a good idea. You should always have at least one other person with you.'

'OK,' Lucy agreed quickly.

'I mean it, Lucy,' Xanthe said and Lucy saw that her eyes, usually so friendly, looked very serious. 'Stardust spirits should not work alone. That way darkness lies.' Her words seemed to hang heavily in the air.

Lucy frowned. What did Xanthe mean? What darkness? She didn't dare ask. She had a feeling she had only just escaped being in trouble already that night and she didn't want to push her luck any further.

Xanthe spoke briskly. 'Well, I'll just clear away this smoke and then I'll follow you home. My work is done here tonight.' She cast another glance in the direction the cat had gone. 'I think,' she said, half under her breath.

Wondering what she meant, Lucy rose into the sky and began to fly home.

As she swooped over the fields Xanthe's words faded, and the memory of the magic she had done before Xanthe arrived filled her mind. A smile pulled at her mouth. It might have been wrong to go back into the woods and use magic on her own but it had felt amazing.

I'll do it again, she realized. *I have to.*

At nine o'clock the next morning, Allegra and Xanthe came round. Dressed in her everyday clothes – a long purple floaty skirt and a short black T-shirt, and with her long blonde hair tied back with a scarf, Xanthe looked very different from the night before, but Lucy felt herself blushing as Xanthe's eyes caught hers and a shared memory of the incident the night before seemed to flash between them. Lucy wondered whether Xanthe had told Allegra, but Allegra didn't send her any curious looks and she didn't mention it when they were alone.

Lucy was glad. She still felt uncomfortable when she thought about Xanthe catching her in the woods on her own.

'Shall we go and see Thumper?' Allegra asked as soon as she had dumped her bag in Lucy's room.

Lucy nodded. Thumper was her rabbit. 'His hutch needs cleaning out. Do you mind helping?'

'Of course not,' Allegra said. Like Lucy, she loved everything to do with animals.

They ran downstairs. There was a chill to the breeze that morning and by the time they had put Thumper into his run and cleaned out the dirty straw their fingers were freezing. As Lucy turned to get some clean straw, she stiffened. All her senses felt suddenly alert.

She swung round.

'What is it?' Allegra asked curiously.

'I don't know,' Lucy replied. 'I just feel odd.' A picture of her rabbit flashed through her mind. 'Thumper!' she exclaimed. Suddenly she had a really strong feeling that something was wrong. She began to run across the garden to where his run was sited.

'No!' she cried out as her eyes took in what was happening.

Thumper was crouched against the ground, trembling in fear as a large black cat prowled around the run, its tail flicking.

Hearing Lucy's cry, the cat looked up. The instant their eyes met, Lucy

felt a jolt of recognition. It was the cat from the night before! She didn't know why but she suddenly felt terrified. She raced towards the cat. 'Get away from Thumper!' she cried, icy fingers running up and down her spine. 'Get away!'

Three

The cat raced away and leapt on to the
high brick wall that separated Lucy's
house from Lavender Cottage.
Crouching down, it stared at Lucy. Its
green eyes seemed to gleam with
cunning and slyness.

'Go on! Shoo!' Lucy shouted. She
loved cats usually, but for some reason

she just felt she wanted this one as far away from her as possible.

The cat jumped down and disappeared into the next-door garden.

Lucy swung round. Poor Thumper. He must have been so scared. Allegra had lifted him out of his run. He was nestled in her arms, his whiskers twitching, his chocolate-coloured ears flattened against his head.

Lucy hurried over and Allegra handed Thumper to her. 'Here. He's fine. He just had a bit of a shock.'

Lucy buried her face in his soft fur. 'Poor boy.'

'Where did that cat come from?' Allegra asked curiously. 'I've never seen it before.'

'I have,' Lucy said. 'I saw it . . .' She broke off, realizing that Allegra didn't know about her visit to the woods the night before. 'I saw it yesterday,' she said vaguely. To her relief Allegra didn't ask when and where. 'I don't like it,' she said with a shiver.

Allegra nodded. 'I know what you mean. When it was on the wall I got this really cold, goosebumpy feeling.'

'Me too!' Lucy exclaimed, relieved her friend had felt the same.

'I wonder where it lives?' Allegra's eyes widened as she had an idea. 'Maybe it belongs to your new neighbours.'

Lucy's heart sank. The last thing she wanted was that cat living next door.

They put Thumper back in his run with some rabbit treats to help him feel better and then they went to the wall to see if they could see the cat in the garden. There was no sign of it.

'Maybe it doesn't live here,' Lucy said hopefully.

Just then the back door opened and a woman came out. She looked about forty and was small and slim with a smiling face and glossy dark hair tucked behind her ears. She saw the girls before they could duck away. 'Hello!' she called cheerfully.

'Hi,' Lucy said, feeling embarrassed at being caught peering over the wall.

'I'm Maggie Chambers,' the woman said, coming over. 'I've just moved in here.'

'I'm Lucy,' Lucy explained. 'And this is Allegra.'

'I live in Willow Cottage,' Allegra added. 'I'm just staying with Lucy.'

'Nice to meet you both,' Maggie smiled. 'I was wondering who our neighbours were.'

Allegra smiled back at Maggie. 'Do you have any children?'

Maggie shook her head. 'No, I'm afraid not. It's just Miss Graves and me. She's eighty and I'm her carer. That means I live with her and help look after her. Oh yes, and of course there's Meg, my cat. She's black with green eyes. You might see her around.'

Lucy's heart sank. So the cat *did* live next door.

Just then the nearest downstairs windows rattled opened and an old lady looked out. Lucy started. She looked just like a witch. Her wispy grey hair was caught back in a bun and her head looked somehow shrunken. Her skin was very wrinkled and dotted with brown liver spots. Her hands reached out of the window, gnarled and claw-like. 'I want my dust!' she exclaimed, her thin old voice high and cracking. 'My dust!' Her blue eyes, faded and red-rimmed, came to rest on Lucy and Allegra. 'Give me my dust!' she cried desperately.

Lucy and Allegra looked at Maggie in alarm.

'Don't worry,' Maggie told them comfortingly. 'Miss Graves is a bit confused because of the move.' She turned. 'It's all right, Miss Graves,' she said brightly. 'Don't get upset.'

'My dust!' The old lady's voice was now a hoarse croak.

Maggie shot a look at the girls. 'I'd better go. See you around.' She hurried into the house. A moment later, Lucy and Allegra saw Miss Graves being taken from the window and the window firmly shut.

Lucy turned from the wall. 'So they're our new neighbours,' she said slowly. She felt slightly shaky. She didn't know why. *It was probably just seeing that old lady like that*, she told herself.

As usual, Allegra spoke what Lucy would have been too tactful to say. 'Miss Graves is really creepy, isn't she? All that stuff about dust – what was she going on about?'

'She's just old,' Lucy said. 'Old people get confused.' She could remember her grandma being like that before she had died.

'I'm glad I'm not Maggie,' Allegra said with a shiver. 'I wouldn't like to look after her. She looked just like a witch.'

'I know,' Lucy admitted. 'Maggie seems nice, though, doesn't she?'

Allegra nodded. 'Pity about her cat. You're going to have to be careful with Thumper.'

Lucy nodded. 'I'll get Dad to see if we can move his run closer to the house.' She looked round. 'We should finish cleaning his hutch and then he can go back in there. At least that's safe.'

They finished getting the hutch ready. As they were putting Thumper back inside, Mrs Evans came out of the house. 'I've just made some chocolate chip cookies. Would you two like some?'

'Yes please!' Lucy and Allegra chorused.

They followed her into the house.

'You must be freezing,' Mrs Evans said as she poured them out drinks of apple juice and handed round the tin of still-warm cookies. 'You've been outside for ages.'

'We met one of our new neighbours,' Lucy told her. 'She's called Maggie. There are two of them. Maggie and an old lady called Miss Graves.'

Her mum looked interested. 'I was planning to pop round later today and take some of these cookies as a welcome present. You two can come along too.'

Lucy felt very reluctant. 'Do we have to?'

'Yes,' Mrs Evans said. 'It's the polite thing to do.'

Lucy knew there was no point in arguing. Her mum and dad were very strict on being polite and having good manners. Sometimes she wished her parents were more like Xanthe, who let Allegra do pretty much what she wanted. 'OK,' she sighed. 'We'll come.'

CHAPTER
Four

Maggie was delighted to see them that afternoon. 'How lovely of you all to call round,' she said after Mrs Evans had introduced herself. 'Do come in, and thank you so much for the biscuits.'

Lucy followed her mum and Allegra into the narrow hall. The walls were pale but the furniture was all dark and old-fashioned. Although Maggie and Miss Graves had only been there a day, it already had the feeling of being an old person's house. There were pictures of cats on the walls and when Lucy peeped into the dining room as they passed, she saw lots of ornaments on the mantelpiece.

Maggie led the way into the lounge. It looked out on to the gardens. Miss Graves was sitting in a high-backed red armchair, a blanket tucked over her knees. Her face looked almost skull-like and, once again, Lucy was reminded of a witch.

Maggie spoke brightly. 'Miss Graves, these are our new neighbours.'

The old lady didn't say anything; she just looked at them with her faded blue eyes.

Maggie smiled at Mrs Evans. 'She's
not quite herself at the moment. Tell
you what, I'll go and get us all a nice
cup of tea.'

She left the room.

Mrs Evans stepped forward. 'Hello, Miss Graves,' she said pleasantly. 'I'm Carol. I live next door with my husband and our three daughters, Rachel, Hope and Lucy. Lucy's the youngest.' She put her hand on Lucy's arm and Lucy stepped forward. She felt really awkward standing there in the silence. 'And this is Allegra Greenwood, who lives next door to us. She's staying at our house for the weekend.'

Lucy felt an icy chill run across her skin and she swung round. The cat was looking round the door. It gazed at her for a moment and then turned and slunk away. Lucy shivered. She really didn't like that cat.

A few moments later Maggie came

back. 'Here we are,' she said cheerfully, bringing in a trolley with teacups, two glasses of orange squash and a plate of rich tea biscuits. 'Do sit down.'

Mrs Evans sat in the armchair next to Miss Graves. Lucy and Allegra perched on the sofa. Lucy fiddled with her watch strap as Maggie poured out the tea. The air of the room felt as if it was pressing down on her.

She took the glass of squash that Maggie handed her. 'Thank you,' she said, forcing the words out.

Maggie sat down on the other side of Mrs Evans. 'So do you work?' Maggie asked Mrs Evans.

Mrs Evans began telling them about her job as a maths teacher.

How long are we going to have to stay?

Lucy thought, glancing at a carriage clock in a nearby glass cabinet. As well as the clock, the cabinet had lots of ornaments and strange objects. One in particular caught Lucy's eye. It was a large glass ball standing on a dark pedestal. It seemed to contain golden, glowing light. Almost without realizing what she was doing, Lucy stood up and went over to it. Peering at it, she saw that the light was really lots of tiny golden grains, swirling around. What was making the dust swirl? Was there some sort of electric current? She reached out to touch it.

'My dust!' Miss Graves suddenly exclaimed.

Lucy jumped. The old lady had struggled up from her chair and was walking towards her, her hand outstretched. 'My dust,' she said in a cracked, desperate voice. 'I want my dust!'

Her fingers closed like a claw on the sleeve of Lucy's jumper. 'Give me my dust.'

Lucy looked at her mum in alarm, but the next second Maggie was there beside her. 'I'm sorry, Lucy,' she said quickly. 'Come on now, Miss Graves,' she said, gently prising Miss Graves's fingers away from Lucy's clothes. 'Come and sit down, dear.'

The desperate look faded from Miss Graves's eyes and she let herself be led away back to her armchair.

'I'm sorry,' Maggie murmured to Mrs Evans as Miss Graves sat back down.

Mrs Evans smiled understandingly. 'It's a big upheaval to move house.'

Feeling shaken, Lucy glanced at Allegra. To her surprise, she saw that Allegra was looking very pale and there was a look of something like fear in her eyes.

Lucy frowned in concern. 'Are you OK?'

Allegra shook her head. 'I . . . I don't feel very well.'

Mrs Evans looked over in concern. 'What's the matter, Allegra?'

'I . . . I feel sick,' Allegra stammered.

'Come on then,' Mrs Evans said, getting quickly to her feet. 'Let's get you home. Maybe you're coming down with a tummy bug or something.' She smiled at Miss Graves. 'It was lovely meeting you. You must come round to our house next time.' The old lady nodded vaguely. Saying a hurried goodbye to Maggie, Mrs Evans and the girls left.

As they walked down the drive, Lucy glanced round. The curtains of one of the windows twitched as if someone had suddenly moved away.

'How are you feeling now?' Mrs Evans asked Allegra.

'I don't feel sick any more but I've got a headache,' Allegra replied weakly.

'In that case I think you should go upstairs and have a rest for a bit,' Mrs Evans said.

Allegra shot a look at Lucy. Lucy immediately knew that she wanted to talk to her – alone.

Unfortunately, when they got back to Jasmine Cottage, Mrs Evans insisted that Allegra should have some rest, and she made Lucy come downstairs with her to help her make lunch.

Reluctantly, Lucy did as she was told. Mrs Evans started getting out bread and ham and cheese. 'We'll have toasted sandwiches for lunch. Can you get out the sandwich toaster, please?'

Lucy fetched the sandwich toaster and plugged it in.

'It was nice meeting our new neighbours,' Mrs Evans said as she began to butter the bread.

Nice wasn't the word Lucy would have chosen. 'Miss Graves is creepy,' she said with a shiver.

Her mum looked cross. 'Lucy! You

should be more respectful towards old people. I know Miss Graves is old and seems a bit confused but she's just moved house and it'll probably take her a while to adjust.'

Lucy didn't say anything. Her mum could say what she liked but Miss Graves was definitely odd. She changed the subject. 'Should I go and ask Allegra what she wants for lunch?'

'All right,' her mum said. 'But tell her she doesn't need to have anything if she doesn't want, and don't stay for long.'

Thankful, Lucy escaped. She opened her bedroom door. Allegra was pacing round the room. She stopped guiltily as the door opened but relaxed when she saw that it was just Lucy.

'Are you OK?' Lucy demanded,

shutting the door behind her. 'What's up?'

'Oh, Lucy,' Allegra said, hurrying over to her and grabbing her hands. 'What are we going to do?'

'About what?' Lucy said, feeling alarmed. She'd never seen Allegra look so worried.

'About Miss Graves,' Allegra gabbled. 'Didn't you see the globe filled with dust? Didn't you feel the strangeness in the air?'

'Yes,' Lucy said slowly. 'So?'

'Isn't it obvious?' Allegra stared at her. 'Miss Graves is a dark stardust spirit!'

Lucy frowned. 'A what?'

'A dark stardust spirit,' Allegra repeated in a frightened whisper.

CHAPTER

Five

Lucy stared at Allegra. 'What's a dark stardust spirit?'

'They're stardust spirits who have turned bad,' Allegra replied. 'They get so tempted by power that they stop working with other stardust spirits and stop doing good. All they want is to get more power. They'll do anything to get it, including . . .' she swallowed, 'taking the stardust from other stardust spirits.'

'What do you mean?' Lucy demanded.

'They have these magic orbs,' Allegra told her. 'They capture normal stardust spirits, hold the orb to their foreheads and say a spell. The stardust leaves the spirit and enters the orb. The dark spirit then controls it and can use it when they want.'

'And what about the stardust spirit the stardust was taken from?' Lucy wasn't sure she wanted to hear the answer.

Allegra bit her lip. 'They can't *ever* become a stardust spirit again. Without their stardust they have to stay trapped in their human body all the time. They remember what being a stardust spirit was like but they can't become one. It's awful. Can you imagine knowing about stardust but not being able to turn into a spirit?'

Lucy couldn't imagine it. It was just too horrible for words. 'But what's this got to do with Miss Graves?' she demanded. 'She can't be a dark spirit. She's old and frail.'

'I know, and that *is* weird. Dark spirits normally use their power to stay young – but I'm sure she's a dark spirit,' Allegra said. 'I had such an odd feeling when I was in the house. Didn't you?' Lucy nodded. 'Then there was the orb in the cabinet,' Allegra went on. 'The glass ball, the one with the dust in. I'm sure that was a magic orb.'

'So all that golden dust was stardust!' Lucy exclaimed. 'What are we going to do?'

'I need to talk to Xanthe,' decided Allegra. 'I'll call her on her mobile.'

As they hurried downstairs, Mrs Evans came out of the kitchen. 'Are you feeling better, Allegra?'

'Yes thanks,' Allegra replied politely. 'Is it all right if I ring my mum?'

'Well, lunch is ready,' Mrs Evans said. 'Why don't you ring her afterwards?'

Allegra didn't have much choice but to agree. She and Lucy went into the kitchen. Lucy realized she had lost her appetite and the bread tasted like cardboard in her mouth.

A dark spirit, she thought. *A dark spirit is living next door.* She had to agree with Allegra that everything Allegra knew about dark spirits seemed to fit with Miss Graves. Lucy remembered the way she kept saying, 'Give me my dust.'

Maybe she was sensing that we're stardust spirits, Lucy thought in alarm. *Maybe she wanted our stardust!*

She couldn't wait to finish lunch so they could ring Xanthe.

Unfortunately, when they made the phone call Lucy's mum was pottering about nearby and Allegra couldn't say anything at all about Miss Graves and their suspicions.

'We'll have to tell some of the other adults tonight,' Lucy whispered to Allegra as they went upstairs.

Allegra nodded. 'We can tell

Rebecca. She's Xanthe's friend. She'll
know what to do.'

Ella and Faye were sitting in the
branches of the oak tree when Lucy
and Allegra flew into the clearing at
the heart of the woods where the
stardust spirits met each night.

'Hi there!' Faye called. She
immediately noticed their tense faces.
'What's up?'

'Lots,' Allegra replied. She quickly
explained about Miss Graves.

Faye and Ella were shocked. 'Let's tell
Rebecca straight away,' Ella urged.

Rebecca was standing by the old oak
in the centre of the clearing, talking
with two other adults – Tom and
Adam. Rebecca was a summer spirit

like Lucy and wore a beautiful golden dress. 'Hi, girls,' she said as they went over to her. 'Do you want something?'

'Yes!' The words burst out of Allegra. 'We think a dark spirit has moved in next door to Lucy!'

The effect on the adults was immediate. Their faces creased in alarm.

'A dark spirit?' Rebecca said quickly. 'Tell us everything.'

Lucy and Allegra explained all about their visit to Miss Graves's house that afternoon, about the uncomfortable feeling they had when they were inside the house and about the glass orb filled with swirling golden dust in the cabinet.

'OK, I'll check this out in the

morning,' Rebecca said when they had finished. 'I live in the village so I can call in and introduce myself on the grounds of being neighbourly.' She shook her head. 'Xanthe said she had a strange feeling the other night.'

'How will you tell if Miss Graves *is* a dark spirit?' Lucy asked.

'It's usually obvious,' Rebecca replied. 'If you're near a dark spirit, you get this feeling that you're being suffocated. It's all to do with the force of the magic that surrounds them. They're so powerful, their magic blocks other people's.' She saw their alarmed faces. 'Look, try not to worry about it,' she said. 'At least you've warned us so we can be on our guard, and by tomorrow we should know the truth.'

They nodded and flew off.

'Scary!' Faye said, as they stopped by the trees at the far side of the clearing.

'Yeah,' Ella agreed. 'Just think, the dark spirit might be out there.' She looked into the shadowy trees behind them.

'Let's not think about it,' Lucy said quickly. 'How about we play hide and seek?'

The others nodded. 'Should . . . should we just stay here in the clearing?' Faye suggested, and from the way she spoke Lucy was sure that she was feeling worried about the thought of a dark spirit roaming the woods in search of stardust.

'All right,' she agreed. 'I'll be on.'

She shut her eyes and counted to thirty while the others hid by camouflaging themselves. All stardust spirits had the ability to camouflage themselves – blending into the background, and making it seem as if they had vanished. But if you looked very carefully you could see the air shimmering slightly in the shape of a person. Lucy found Faye camouflaged against the oak tree and Allegra camouflaged against the starry sky. It was harder to find Ella, who was very good at camouflaging herself, but at last Lucy spotted the telltale shimmering of the air in front of a holly bush.

'Found you!' she cried, swooping down.

Ella laughed. 'Who's on now?'

'Me!' said Faye. 'I was found first.' She shut her eyes and began counting.

Lucy quickly flew to an aspen tree on the far side of the clearing. It had a wide trunk and on the floor around it was a thick layer of golden leaves that had fallen from its branches. She sat down on the leaves, curled herself into as small a ball as possible and concentrated on making herself blend in against the tree's ridged grey trunk. It was much harder to stay properly camouflaged if you didn't move around but she thought she could probably manage it if she concentrated. When she was sure she was invisible, she sat very still.

Above her the leaves rustled and trembled. Lucy had heard aspen trees being called 'the whispering trees' and it really did sound as if the leaves were whispering to each other. Xanthe had told her and Allegra that in the old days people had thought that aspen trees were gateways to fairyland. There were legends about their trunks opening up and people following fairies inside. Lucy shivered. She'd thought the stories were just made up but maybe the fairies in the stories had been dark spirits and the people really *had* disappeared into the tree trunks.

Across the clearing Lucy saw Faye finding Ella in the branches of the oak tree. A breeze blew across her face, shaking the leaves that were still clinging to the beech's half-bare branches. Several leaves twisted free. They began to float down to the ground. Lucy watched them as they spun gently in the breeze – golden, red and brown . . .

As she followed their progress from the branch to the ground a warmth began to flood through her. *Golden, red*

and brown. The colours seemed to swirl around her. For one moment she almost felt she knew what it was like to be a leaf, to bud and grow, to flutter in a spring breeze, to feel the warmth of the sun and finally to float down to the ground where you would lie still forever . . .

'Stop!' she whispered, staring intently at the leaf, the words coming out before she really realized what she was saying.

The leaf stopped in mid-air. It hovered about a metre above the grass.

Lucy blinked in surprise.

The leaf immediately swirled round and began to head for the ground.

Stop! Lucy thought again.

The leaf halted. It quivered in the air, pulled down by gravity but kept in place by Lucy's magic.

Lucy was so astonished that she forgot to concentrate on her camouflage.

'Found you!' Faye cried from above her.

Lucy looked round as Allegra and Ella came swooping towards her.

'What happened?' Faye said. 'I could see you easily!' She broke off as she saw the startled look on Lucy's face.

'Is something the matter?' she said
quickly.

'I . . . I . . .' Lucy couldn't explain.
'Watch this!' She found a breeze
twirling a leaf gently to the ground.
'Look at that leaf,' she said, pointing.

She stared at it and tried to find the
same feelings in her mind. The leaf
spun round, orange and red. Lucy
concentrated on it but also let herself
relax. Warm magic from all around
began to flow into her. The rest of the
world seemed to fade away . . .

Stop! Lucy thought.

The leaf hovered in mid-air just as
the first leaf had done.

Lucy heard all her friends give a
sharp intake of breath. She let the leaf
drop and then caught it again with her

mind. Three times she stopped it before letting it fall to the ground.

'But . . . but . . . how did you do that?' Ella said.

'I don't know,' Lucy told her. 'I was just sitting here watching the leaves and it happened. I thought *stop* – and the leaf I was looking at stopped.'

'Weird,' Faye said.

Lucy looked at Allegra, hoping for an explanation. 'Some stardust spirits *can* stop things falling,' Allegra said. 'It's like an extra power. Not many spirits can do it, though, and I've never heard of anyone our age being able to do it.' She gave Lucy a strange, almost wary look.

Lucy looked at Faye and Ella. They were looking at her as if she was some kind of creature from outer space again.

Just then Rebecca flew over. 'Hi, girls. Can I get you to do a job for us?' She saw their faces. 'Is everything OK?' she asked curiously.

'Yes . . . er, fine,' Lucy stammered.

'Lucy's just discovered she can stop things falling,' Allegra said slowly, her eyes not leaving Lucy's face.

Rebecca stared. 'Really? That's wonderful, Lucy! Not many spirits can do that. Let's see.'

Lucy showed her how she could stop the leaves from falling. 'Goodness!' Rebecca said in amazement. 'Come on, you must show the others!'

She led Lucy over to the oak tree and Lucy performed her magic all over

again for the other adults – Adam,
Sasha, Laura and Tom. Now she knew
what she had to do, it was getting
easier and easier to enter the right state
of mind for the magic to flow in. She
stopped a nut that Adam threw into
the air, and then stopped five leaves
together. As she let the leaves drop, she
felt almost dizzy with power. Looking
at the astonishment on the adults' faces,
she grinned. It felt great to have them
looking at her like that.

'I've never known someone so
young be able to stop things falling,'
Sasha said, sounding very impressed.
'And to stop them so easily. Normally
it takes years of practice.'

'How do you do it?' Laura asked Lucy.

'It just sort of happens,' she

explained. 'I just look at the thing and say *stop* with my mind.'

The adults exchanged glances.

'You have a lot of power, Lucy,' Tom said slowly. 'In fact, a quite amazing amount for someone your age. As you get older and learn more about magic, you may well find you have other powers too.'

'What sort of powers?' Lucy asked eagerly.

'Like being able to talk to animals or being able to see far into the distance, beyond the reach of human eyes,' Tom replied. 'There are all sorts of other powers that stardust spirits can have.'

Rebecca nodded. 'Magic is all around us. As you get older you will learn to draw on all the magic in the natural world. You will work to understand the rustle of the wind, the gurgling of the river, the swish of grass. All stardust spirits train to be able to draw on this magic as they get older but it is usually only the most powerful who master it.'

'I saw Xanthe talking to some birds once,' Lucy said, remembering. 'Do you think I'll be able to do that one day?'

Rebecca looked at her for a moment. 'With the power you have, Lucy, I think you'll be able to do anything you want,' she said solemnly.

Lucy stared at her. Was she joking? But Rebecca's eyes were deadly serious and looking round at the other adults, Lucy saw they were nodding too.

Delight swept through her. She suddenly wanted to jump and shout in excitement. She just about stopped herself but she couldn't hold back the grin that spread across her face. Glancing round she saw the others watching nearby. Rebecca followed her gaze. 'Go on, go back to your friends. It would be good if you could all go and check on the badgers' set near the hornbeam grove tonight.'

'OK,' Lucy said. She raced back to the others, her heart singing.

'So what did they say?' Faye demanded.

'They were really impressed,' Lucy said. 'They told me I'm going to be mega powerful and that there's a whole load of other powers I might develop. Isn't it cool?'

'Yeah!' Faye said.

Neither Allegra nor Ella spoke.

Lucy looked at them. They didn't look exactly pleased for her.

Maybe they're jealous, she thought suddenly. She wondered how she would have felt if either of them had developed new powers that she didn't have. *Probably not great*, she admitted to herself. 'Of course, Rebecca and the others said it's going to take ages for me to develop new powers. Years, probably,' she added quickly.

Ella looked a bit happier. 'Oh right, so it's just this stopping thing you can do.'

Lucy nodded. 'Yeah. I bet I won't be able to do anything else.'

Allegra didn't look totally convinced.

Wanting everything to be back to

normal, Lucy hastily changed the
subject. 'Anyway, they want us to go
and check the badgers near the
hornbeam grove. Come on, I'll race

you there!' She plunged into the air.

'Not fair. You've got a head start!'
Ella called.

'Wait, Lucy!' Faye shouted.

'No way,' Lucy cried. 'Catch me if
you can!' She raced away.

It was as if her new powers had
been forgotten. Laughing and shouting,
the others charged after her as she
swooped through the trees. But at the
back of Lucy's mind, Rebecca's words
repeated themselves. *With the power you
have inside you, I think you'll be able to
do anything you want.*

Lucy suppressed a grin. *Cool!* she
thought.

CHAPTER

Six

When Lucy and Allegra got home that
night, Allegra fell asleep almost straight
away but Lucy lay awake, reliving the
moment in the clearing when she'd
been doing her new magic for the
adults. It had felt good – more than
good. It had felt fantastic. To have
everyone watching her and telling her
she was powerful, to feel the magic

flowing through her and know she could do things others couldn't. Lucy hugged herself. The idea that she might also have even more magic powers was wonderful.

Glancing at the window, Lucy looked out at the stars. Regulus was near the horizon. It seemed to pull Lucy's gaze towards it and she smiled. She loved being a summer spirit and being able to do summer magic. Her eyes drifted across the other stars. In the centre of the sky another bright star shone out.

Aldebaran, Lucy thought, tracing the shape of the bull constellation that the Royal Star, Aldebaran, was part of. Spring spirits' stardust came from Aldebaran and it gave them their powers. As Lucy looked into its brightness, she felt herself wondering for the first time, what it would be like to draw on its magic. How did it feel to make things grow like Ella could? Or make the wind blow like Allegra? Or make it rain or hail like Faye?

For a moment, Lucy imagined drawing on the power of all the four Royal Stars – not just having the magic of one star but having the magic of them all. She could almost feel the crackle of magic, feel power sweeping over her . . .

Shutting her eyes she let herself imagine what it would be like and slowly, slowly she drifted into sleep.

★

Lucy was woken up the next day by the sound of Allegra getting out of bed.

'Morning,' Allegra said, stretching. She went to the window. 'It looks lovely outside,' she said looking out at the crisp blue sky. 'What are we going to do today?'

'I don't know . . .' Lucy started to reply but she broke off as Allegra took a sharp intake of breath. 'What is it?'

'The cat's sitting on the wall,' Allegra said, stepping back from the window. 'It's looking up here. It's like it's watching us.'

Lucy jumped out of bed and went to the window.

Allegra was right. Meg was sitting on the wall, her green eyes staring straight at Lucy's bedroom window.

'It gives me the creeps,' Allegra said with a shiver. 'She doesn't act like a cat should.'

A horrid thought struck Lucy. 'Maybe it's not really a cat. Maybe it's Miss Graves disguised! Can dark spirits do that?' she asked anxiously. 'Change into animals, I mean?'

'They can.' Allegra looked alarmed. 'It takes a lot of power but they can do it. You could be right!' But then she shook her head. 'No, no it can't be her. Remember when we were at Miss Graves's house, she and the cat were on the same room? Do you remember – it came in when Maggie was making the tea?'

'Oh yeah,' Lucy said. She felt relieved. 'So it's not Miss Graves, but maybe it's spying on us for her. She might be able to talk to it.'

Allegra nodded. 'I'm glad Rebecca's coming round today. The sooner the adults realize that Miss Graves is a dark spirit the better.'

'I know,' Lucy agreed.

All morning they kept an eye on the house next door. Nothing unusual happened. At one point, Maggie came out into the garden and hung some washing on the line. And a little while later they heard the front door of Lavender Cottage opening.

'Maybe Miss Graves is going out,' Allegra hissed.

They hurried round to the front of Jasmine Cottage. But it was just

Maggie. She seemed in a bit of a rush, pulling her coat on while she hurried down the path, but she smiled when she saw them. 'Hi, girls. What are you up to today?'

Spying on your house, Lucy thought, but she just shrugged. 'Nothing much.'

'Well, I'm just going shopping,' Maggie said, putting a bag into the car. 'See you later.' She got into her car, started the engine and drove off quickly.

Lucy and Allegra were just heading back round to the back of the house when they heard footsteps on the gravel. They looked round and saw Rebecca walking up the path.

'Hi, R–' Lucy started to say, but then her dad came out to do some gardening and she broke off. He didn't know she knew Rebecca and it would be too difficult to explain.

Rebecca shot them a quick smile and continued on to the front door. She rang the bell.

'You two look at a loose end. Are you going to help me do some gardening?' Mr Evans said.

Lucy hesitated. It would give them an excuse to watch the house and see Rebecca when she came out. 'OK,' she agreed.

'Great. I'll go and fetch you a bucket and you can do some weeding for me,' Mr Evans said.

He went off.

Lucy and Allegra watched as the door to Lavender Cottage slowly opened. Miss Graves stood in the doorway, looking uncertainly at Rebecca.

They were too far away to hear the conversation but they saw Rebecca talking and smiling as she introduced herself and Miss Graves nod and say something. Then Rebecca went into the house and the door shut.

'I hope she's OK,' Lucy said. 'She'll be on her own with Miss Graves.'

Allegra looked worried. 'I hadn't thought of that. I wish Maggie hadn't gone out.' She bit her lip. 'What shall we do?'

'Watch the place I guess,' Lucy replied. 'If she hasn't come out in twenty minutes I reckon we should go and knock on the door.'

'OK,' Allegra agreed.

Just then Mr Evans returned with a bucket, two trowels, two pairs of gloves and a mat to kneel on. 'Here you go,' he said cheerfully.

Lucy and Allegra chose a place in the garden that gave them a clear view of Lavender Cottage. As the minutes ticked by, Lucy felt her nerves starting to tighten. Rebecca was OK, wasn't she? She checked her watch. It had been ten minutes since they had seen Rebecca go into the house.

'Lucy, that's a geranium, not a weed!' Mr Evans exclaimed as Lucy pulled a clump of green leaves out of the ground.

'Oh . . . sorry,' Lucy said, looking at the plant guiltily. She hadn't been concentrating at all. 'I'll plant it again,' she told her dad.

He sighed. 'I'm really grateful to you both for helping me but can you please try and be more careful?'

Lucy nodded but her mind wasn't on the gardening. Minutes crept by. Lucy checked her watch again. Eighteen minutes had now passed since Rebecca had gone inside.

'We're going to have to do something,' Allegra whispered to Lucy.

Lucy swallowed nervously. The last thing she felt like doing was going to knock on Miss Graves's door, but Rebecca could be in trouble. She glanced across at her dad. He was pruning back an overgrown shrub.

'Dad, can I have some more gloves, please?' she said, secretly dipping her gloves in a muddy puddle. 'These have got a bit wet.'

'No problem,' her dad said, putting his secateurs down. 'I've got plenty of other gloves in the shed. I'll go and fetch you another pair.'

He headed round the back of the house.

Lucy took a deep breath. 'OK,' she said in a tense voice to Allegra. 'Let's go.'

They had taken two steps towards the driveway when the front door opened and Rebecca came out.

Lucy's relief was so strong that she almost had to sit down. Rebecca looked fine. She was smiling at Miss Graves and as she left, she patted the old lady on the arm. Lucy strained her ears. Rebecca seemed to be saying something about seeing her again soon.

'Rebecca's all right,' Allegra breathed.

Rebecca turned and started walking

down the path. As she passed the girls, she smiled and shook her head faintly. Then she was gone and Miss Graves had shut the front door again.

'She shook her head,' Lucy whispered to Allegra.

'I know,' Allegra said. 'What do you think she meant?'

'I don't know but she looked quite cheerful,' Lucy frowned. 'Maybe Miss Graves isn't a dark spirit, after all.'

'But she is!' Allegra protested. 'You saw the orb. You know how odd it was in that house. There was danger there, I know there was.'

Lucy didn't need convincing. She had definitely felt the presence of a dark spirit next door too. But then why had Rebecca been looking so relaxed as she left? And what had Rebecca's shake of her head meant?

Her dad came back into the garden with the gloves. Lucy sighed with frustration. It looked like they'd just have to wait till that evening to find out.

CHAPTER
Seven

It seemed to take ages for Lucy's family to all go to bed that night but at last silence fell in the Evanses' house. 'OK,' Lucy whispered. 'Let's go now!'

She and Allegra jumped out of bed and opened the window. A cool breeze blew across their skin.

'I believe in stardust,' they both whispered. 'I believe in stardust. *I believe in stardust!*'

As the last word left Lucy's mouth, she felt warmth flood through her. She and Allegra twirled upwards, flying out of the window; their pyjamas transformed into their glittering stardust dresses.

Freedom! Lucy thought as she felt the starlight falling on her skin.

'We should camouflage ourselves,' Allegra said, glancing nervously at Lavender Cottage. 'Just in case Miss Graves or the cat are watching.'

'Camouflagus,' they both whispered and instantly they faded into the background of the night sky.

'Come on!' Lucy exclaimed. 'I want to find Rebecca!'

Rebecca was waiting for them. 'I'm glad you're here. I need to talk to you about Miss Graves.'

Lucy felt her throat tighten. 'She's a dark spirit, isn't she?'

'No,' Rebecca answered. 'She's not. I didn't get any sense of dark magic around her at all.' She looked at Lucy and Allegra reassuringly. 'She's just a normal old lady, a bit confused maybe, but normal.'

Lucy and Allegra stared.

'But . . .' Lucy stammered, feeling totally taken aback. She'd been convinced that Miss Graves was a dark spirit. 'But she *can't* be!'

'She is,' Rebecca insisted. 'I'd have sensed it if she'd been a dark spirit.'

'What about the orb?' Allegra demanded.

'Well, I don't know what you saw, but there certainly wasn't an orb there,' Rebecca replied. 'I checked all the cabinets but there were just normal ornaments in them. You must have been mistaken.'

'We weren't!' Allegra exclaimed.

Rebecca squeezed her arm. 'Look, it's really good that you and Lucy are being so alert. But there's no need to worry about Miss Graves.' She smiled at them. 'Anyway, I'd better go.'

She flew off. Lucy felt completely confused. She'd been so sure about Miss Graves being a dark spirit. 'I don't get it,' she said. 'Miss Graves *can't* be normal.'

Allegra nodded. 'We both sensed something was wrong. We both saw that orb.' Her face looked troubled. 'Maybe Miss Graves cast a spell on Rebecca – tricked her into thinking she was good.'

'Could she do that?' Lucy asked in alarm.

'Yes,' Allegra replied. 'Dark spirits are good at playing tricks on people's minds. It can take a very powerful spirit to resist them.'

'Well, I don't believe Miss Graves is normal,' Lucy muttered. 'I think we should still keep an eye on her.'

Allegra nodded in agreement. 'At least until Xanthe comes home. She'll be able to tell if Miss Graves is a dark spirit. I know she will.'

Just then Ella and Faye arrived. Lucy and Allegra filled them in on everything Rebecca had said.

'But we still think there's something weird about Miss Graves,' Allegra finished.

Faye shivered. 'I'm glad she's not living next door to me.'

Allegra glanced at Lucy. 'I think we should practise using our magic powers tonight. We want to make sure we're as strong as possible, just in case.'

'OK,' Lucy agreed.

They headed over to the far side of the clearing. At first Lucy practised protecting things by conjuring a magical shield around them. She

protected a blade of grass and then
tried to get the others to bend it or
break it but they couldn't. Ella, who
had recently discovered that she could
use her magic to clear the ground of
plants as well as to make plants grow,
cleared a patch of grass to bare soil,
grew a patch of snowdrops and then

used her higher powers of disguise to make them look like grass again. Faye conjured a rain cloud and then, as it started raining, she froze the water in the air so that it fell as hail. Allegra conjured a breeze which swept all the fallen leaves in the clearing into the air in a snake-shape, then she made the breeze disappear, leaving them in a neat pile.

Lucy looked at the pile of leaves. The memory of how it had felt to use her normal powers and her higher powers at the same time flashed into her mind. She couldn't resist.

She pointed at the leaves. 'Shield be with me!' Power raced through her, hot and strong. 'Fire be with me!' she breathed next.

A ball of fire burst from her fingers but as it reached the leaves it seemed to hit an invisible barrier and exploded in a cloud of sparks. Lucy laughed in delight.

'Lucy!'

She jumped in surprise and looked round. Ella was staring at her angrily, her hands on her hips. 'You know you're not supposed to do that. It's dangerous!'

'It's not,' Lucy protested. 'I managed fine. I . . .'

'Lucy!'

Rebecca and Tom came hurrying across the clearing towards her. From the look on their faces it was clear they had seen what she was doing. Lucy's heart sank. She was in trouble now.

'Did you just combine your seasonal and your higher powers?' Adam demanded.

'Yes,' Lucy replied, blushing.

'Have you done it before?' Rebecca asked.

'Um . . . yes,' Lucy admitted.

'Well, you shouldn't have,' Rebecca said sternly. 'It can be very dangerous to combine your powers like that. Your magic might easily spiral out of control, endangering not only you but the forest and people around you.'

Lucy hung her head. 'Sorry.'

There was a pause. When Rebecca spoke her voice was softer. 'It's OK, Lucy. You shouldn't have done it, but you managed very well.' Lucy glanced up. There was a new look of respect on Rebecca's face. 'I've never known a spirit your age be able to combine their powers before.'

'Me neither,' Adam put in. 'It was amazing, Lucy. Just don't try it again though,' he added warningly.

'I won't,' Lucy replied. Flashing a relieved smile at them, she flew off to join the others, who were waiting a little way off. 'It's OK,' she said quickly. 'I didn't get told off that much. In fact, Rebecca and Adam seemed really impressed that I could combine my powers.' Happiness bubbled through her as she remembered the admiration in the adults' eyes.

'That's great,' Allegra said but she didn't sound like she meant it.

'Mmm,' Ella said.

They exchanged glances. Suddenly Lucy remembered what she had felt the night before – were they jealous? She hesitated. She was so pleased that the adults thought she was powerful she wanted to talk about it, but she could kind of understand that her friends didn't feel the same way. She bit her lip, not quite sure what to say.

Faye broke the silence by changing the subject. 'Come on, should we play a game or something? How about tick?'

'OK,' Ella said, flying into the air as if she was relieved to have something else to think about. 'Bagsy not be on!'

Lucy shrugged. 'I'll be on. I don't mind.'

They scattered and she started to

chase them through the sky. She caught
Ella first and then Allegra.

'Now for Faye!' Ella called.

Lucy set off after Faye. She seemed
to have taken a leaf out of Allegra's
book and she darted around, always
managing to just escape from their
outstretched hands.

'Can't catch me!' she giggled as she
dived safely past Lucy for the third
time. Lucy exclaimed in exasperation.

'Come and get me, Lucy!' Faye
teased.

Lucy raced towards Faye but Faye
dived again, just managing to avoid
Lucy's fingers. 'Missed!' she called.

Frustration swept over Lucy. Hardly
knowing what she was doing, she raised
her hands. Power tingled through her.

Stop! The thought rang out in her mind.

Faye immediately jerked to a stop in mid-air. Her legs and arms dangled. Her eyes widened and her mouth opened and closed in panic. 'What . . . what's happening?' she gasped.

Lucy could feel magic surging through her. Her skin felt like it was burning hot, but inside she felt almost icily calm as she watched Faye dangling like a puppet on an invisible string. She felt unbelievably powerful and in control . . .

'Lucy, stop it!' Allegra grabbed Lucy's arm.

Lucy started in surprise, breaking the magic. Faye dropped through the air a few metres before realizing she was free.

Lucy looked at Allegra. Her friend's eyes were blazing. 'Lucy! How *could* you? You used magic to control Faye! What were you thinking of?'

Lucy didn't know what to say. Part of her couldn't believe she'd just done what she'd done. But a secret bit of her remembered how good it had felt. *No!* She slammed that thought firmly away. 'I . . . I don't know what happened,' she stammered.

Lucy looked desperately at Faye. Ella had her arm around her shoulders and Faye was crying. Lucy started to fly towards her. 'Faye, I . . .'

'Stay away from her, Lucy!' Ella shouted angrily.

'You're an idiot, Lucy,' Allegra said, sounding disgusted. She flew to join

Ella and Faye. 'Just because you're powerful you think you can do anything. Well, if you're not careful, *you'll* turn into a dark spirit!'

Lucy flinched at Allegra's harsh words. 'No I won't!' She looked at her friends standing all together, shoulder by shoulder. Faye looked utterly shaken and the other two looked furious. 'You're just jealous,' Lucy cried, her guilt at what she had done coming out as anger. 'You hate it that I can do magic like that. That I'm more powerful than all of you!'

A sob choked her. She couldn't bear the way they were looking at her – like they didn't know her at all.

Tears streaming down her face, Lucy spun round and raced away.

CHAPTER

Eight

Lucy flew through the trees as fast as she could. She wanted to fly and fly and never stop. She couldn't believe she'd used magic to control Faye. She glanced behind her. There was no sign of the others. Dashing a hand across her eyes to get rid of the guilty tears that were streaming down her face, she saw an oak tree ahead.

Sniffing hard, she flew to it and sat down in the space where its trunk forked into two. Burying her face in her hands, Lucy let herself cry. Why had she been so stupid? Why had she tried to stop Faye? Why had she said those awful things?

'What have I done?' she sobbed. There was no way the others would ever forgive her now.

The leaves of the tree whispered in the breeze and gradually Lucy's sobs calmed down, as the strength of the old tree seemed to flow into her. Her thoughts steadied. Maybe if she said she was sorry to the others. If she promised never to use magic against anyone again. Then maybe they'd forgive her, maybe . . .

A faint whooshing sound made her look up. Allegra, Ella and Faye were flying towards her.

Allegra stopped. 'Lucy?' She looked tentatively at her. 'Are . . . are you OK?'

Lucy's fingers gripped the tree's bark. This wasn't going to be easy but she knew what she had to say. 'No, I'm not,' she said, swallowing. 'I feel awful.' The words began to tumble out of her. 'I should never have used magic against Faye. It was a horrible thing to do and I should never have said you were jealous of me. I've been really stupid. I'm really, really sorry and I'll never do it again.' Blinking back tears, she looked down at her knees. What would they say?

The next instant she felt a current of air swish past her and Allegra, Ella and Faye landed in the tree beside her.

'Oh, Luce,' Allegra said, putting an arm around her shoulders. 'Don't cry. I'm sorry I said you were going to turn into a dark spirit. I didn't mean it. Look, it's OK.'

'Yes,' Faye said, squeezing her hand. 'I was just shocked.'

Relief rushed through Lucy. She looked at them. 'You're still friends with me then?'

'Of course we are.' Faye managed a small smile. 'Just don't do it again.'

'I won't,' Lucy promised fervently. She glanced at Ella, aware that Ella hadn't spoken.

'It was a dumb thing to do,' Ella said

in her usual blunt way. 'But we're still
friends.'

Lucy let out a long sigh of relief. 'I
thought you were never going to speak

to me again. I didn't mean what I said about you being jealous of me either.'

Ella looked slightly uncomfortable. 'Well, maybe we are a little. It is weird seeing you do all these things and having all the adults saying how great you are.'

Allegra nodded. 'Yeah. It used to be that you could just start fires easily but now you're doing all these new things and it's hard not to be a tiny bit jealous.' She hugged Lucy again. 'But I promise I'll try.'

'I'm not jealous,' Faye put in. 'I'm just scared.'

'Scared!' Lucy echoed in astonishment. 'Of me?'

'You do look rather weird when you do major magic,' Allegra told her. 'Your face goes all like this.' She pulled a strange face and made her eyes all wide and staring.

Lucy shoved her arm. 'I don't!'

Allegra grinned. 'Well, maybe it's more like this.'

She pulled another face. It was so odd that Lucy and the others burst out laughing.

'Idiot!' Lucy grinned.

Faye flew into the air. 'Should we play tick again?'

'OK,' Allegra replied. She grinned at Lucy. 'But *I'll* be on this time.'

The next day was Monday. At half past eight, Lucy and Allegra picked up their school bags and put on their shoes.

'I'm glad Xanthe's coming back tonight,' Lucy said to Allegra.

Allegra nodded. 'She's more powerful than Rebecca. It'll be much harder for Miss Graves to trick her.'

Calling goodbye, they opened the door. As they walked down the path they heard the sound of a window opening.

'It's Miss Graves!' Lucy said in alarm, seeing the old lady at the window.

'She's looking at us!' Allegra said.

Miss Graves's eyes were fastened on them and her face had a look of desperation. 'My dust,' she cried hoarsely. 'I want my dust!'

Allegra began to run down the path, her school bag bumping on her back. Lucy raced after her. As they reached the end of the drive and turned on to the road, there was a rustle in the bushes.

Lucy grabbed Allegra's arm as she saw Meg crouched under a nearby bush. She seemed to be looking almost hungrily at them.

'Come on,' Lucy urged Allegra. 'Let's get out of here!'

It was almost a relief to be at school doing normal things like spellings and maths sheets instead of thinking about dark spirits and spying cats.

'I hope Xanthe's home,' Lucy said when they walked home at the end of the day.

Rounding the corner they saw Xanthe's car in the driveway of Willow

Cottage. 'Mum's back!' Allegra exclaimed. She lowered her voice. 'Let's go and tell her about Miss Graves.'

To their relief, Xanthe took what they said about Miss Graves very seriously. 'I thought something was wrong the other night,' she said. 'I'll go round to Lavender Cottage right now. Do you two want to wait here?'

Lucy and Allegra nodded.

Five minutes later Xanthe came back. 'No one was in but I definitely got a sense of danger when I was near the door. Something's going on.'

'Miss Graves is a dark spirit, I'm sure,' Allegra told her.

'And Meg, the cat, acts as her spy,' Lucy said with a shiver.

'I'll talk to Rebecca,' Xanthe told

them. 'And I'll visit Miss Graves again tomorrow morning. OK?'

Feeling slightly reassured, Lucy and Allegra nodded and then Lucy went home to get changed out of her school clothes.

Going up to her room, she went to the window. A familiar black shape was crouched on the garden wall looking up at her. Meg.

Lucy drew the curtains sharply. Why couldn't Meg leave her alone? A flame of anger flicked through her. It wasn't just her it was affecting. Poor Thumper hadn't been out in his run since Saturday. Although her dad had moved the run closer to the house, whenever Lucy tried to put Thumper down in it, the rabbit began to tremble and try to get out. Lucy didn't blame Thumper for being scared. She didn't trust Meg one little bit either. *It's not fair*, she thought. *Why should Thumper have to stay in his hutch and why should I have to shut my curtains?*

She hesitated and made up her mind. Taking a breath, she pulled the curtains open. Meg stared up at her, but this time Lucy glared back. 'Watch me if you want,' she declared, trying to ignore the shiver that ran across her skin. 'I don't care.'

She turned away from the window. Why did Meg want to spy on her anyway? Miss Graves must already know she was a stardust spirit. What was she trying to find out?

★

When Lucy turned into a stardust spirit that night, Meg was crouching on the wall again.

'Camouflagus,' Lucy whispered, and concentrating hard on keeping herself disguised, she flew out of the window. But as Lucy flew into the sky, Meg's eyes seemed to follow her anyway. The cat stretched, and then, jumping down from the wall, she trotted into the shadows.

Watching her go, Lucy was suddenly filled with the feeling that something bad was going to happen. Out of nowhere panic gripped her and, not stopping to think, she began to fly as fast as she could towards the woods.

As she flew into the trees, her fear faded and she slowed down. Her heart

was hammering but she couldn't say why she'd been so scared.

A faint noise behind her made her glance round. Was someone following her? Her eyes scanned the darkness but there was no one there.

Lucy shivered and, swinging round, she headed as fast as she could for the safety of the clearing.

CHAPTER

Nine

Ella, Allegra and Faye were all waiting
for her. 'Xanthe wants us to go to the
river to check the water voles are OK
and to make sure the water is clear of
litter,' Allegra told her.

'OK,' Lucy agreed. Her heart was still
beating fast after her journey from
home and it was a relief to see
everything in the clearing looking just

like normal. The adults were talking, and a group of teenagers was hanging out in the branches of the oak tree.

'Let's play hide-and-seek on the way there,' Allegra said. 'Come on!'

Ella and Faye agreed enthusiastically but Lucy wasn't really in the mood. As they swooped through the trees, she kept glancing around. She couldn't shake off the feeling that someone was following them.

When they reached the riverbank they found that the colony of water voles was thriving and the river looked to be flowing well. The girls checked along it, picking up litter and clearing away any plants that were too overgrown. As Lucy worked, she felt herself becoming calmer. *I was probably just over-reacting,* she told herself. She was just spooked by the cat spying on her the whole time. *Horrid thing!* she thought, anger flaring through her again.

As she conjured a small fire to burn a pile of rubbish they had collected, her skin prickled. She looked round. Was someone watching her?

'What is it?' Allegra asked from her position just a few feet down the riverbank.

'I don't know,' Lucy said uneasily. 'I've got the weird feeling someone's watching us,'

Allegra frowned. 'I feel something odd too.'

'Do . . . do you think it's a dark spirit?' Faye said, her voice quavering.

'I don't know,' Lucy said, feeling her chest tighten with panic. Was it Miss Graves? Was Miss Graves there? They were quite a long way from the main clearing.

Just then her ears caught a rustle in the bushes to her right. She looked around just in time to see Meg slinking into the undergrowth.

'You!' Lucy exclaimed. The cat looked at her and then slipped away into the shadows.

'Who is it?' Allegra demanded.

'It's Meg!' Lucy replied, her fear turning to anger. 'She's spying again. Well, I've had enough of it. I'm sick of being watched!' She flew up.

'Where are you going?' demanded Allegra.

'After Meg,' Lucy declared.

'But why? What are you going to do?' Ella said in alarm.

Lucy didn't know. She just wanted to chase the cat away – far away. In the distance, Regulus appeared on the horizon. Its starlight shimmered across her skin, sending magic sparking through her. As it combined with her anger, a wave of power swept over her. She could look after herself. She was strong. Everyone said so. 'Maybe I'll catch Meg talking to Miss Graves, and then people are going to *have* to believe that Miss Graves is a dark spirit,' she declared.

'Lucy, don't be stupid,' Allegra said. 'Let's go and find the adults and tell them about Meg spying on us.'

But Lucy felt swept along by a rush of power. 'I'll be OK.'

'Please, don't go, Lucy,' Faye said.

'Don't worry,' Lucy told her reassuringly. 'I won't get into trouble.'

'You can't go on your own,' Allegra protested.

'Yes I can,' Lucy said. She could tell they didn't want to come with her. 'Look, you lot stay here. If I haven't come back in ten minutes, you can come and find me.' She saw the uncertainty on their faces. 'I'll be fine.' She knew she didn't have time to argue. Meg was getting further and further away by the second.

'I'm going,' she declared, and, leaving the others behind, she plunged into the trees after the cat.

She flew swiftly to the next clearing and then hesitated. Meg had been heading northwards towards the village but she could have gone anywhere in the woods.

Lucy tried to let her mind focus. *Cat*, she thought. *Cat* . . .

Her skin tingled and suddenly she felt the weirdest feeling – as if her mind was somehow leaving her body, reaching out to where the cat had gone.

Yes! There! She could sense Meg's presence.

Meg was moving swiftly through the trees but she wasn't heading towards the village. She was going deeper into the woods. Lucy's eyes snapped open and she began to fly as fast as she could after her. Her heart pounded

with excitement as she chased onwards.
Meg couldn't get away. She was going
to catch her!

And then what?

Lucy forced the thought away.
Weaving in and out of the trees, she
pursued the cat, her mind focused on
the chase.

Closer, she thought. *I know I'm getting
closer!*

She reached a grove of hornbeam
trees . . . There she was!

Meg swung round. Her black ears
flattened against her head and she let
out a long low hiss. It was a strange
sound – menacing but also somehow
triumphant.

Lucy paused, a feeling of unease
flickering through her.

The air around Meg started to tremble.

Lucy stared. Meg seemed to be growing bigger! Lucy's heart started to pound. What was happening? In front of her astonished eyes, the cat's black body started to change shape; its body stretched, its front legs became arms, and its head became human . . .

It was turning into a crouching woman.

'No!' Lucy gasped. 'You can't –' She broke off as the woman straightened up and sent a bolt of fire whizzing towards her.

Lucy instinctively ducked but almost immediately realized that the bolt hadn't been sent to hit her but the tree above her. There was a sharp crack and a large branch snapped away from the trunk. It smacked into her back. Crying out in pain, Lucy tumbled through the air, her arms and legs flailing.

Thud!

She landed on the forest floor. For a moment she thought she was never going to breathe again. Gasping painfully, she struggled to draw in some air. Her shoulder throbbed from where the branch had hit it, but it didn't feel broken. She sat up, her eyes darting across the clearing to where the cat had been.

A woman was standing there, a cold cruel smile on her face, her short dark hair gleaming in the starlight.

'No!' Lucy whispered.

It was Maggie.

CHAPTER

Ten

'But you *can't* be the dark spirit,' Lucy gasped, staring at Maggie.

Maggie laughed coldly. Her face looked different; more beautiful and more ancient. 'Can't I?' she said softly.

'No,' Lucy stammered. But suddenly everything was clicking into place. She and Allegra had never seen the cat and Maggie together. Whenever they had felt that icy-cold horrible feeling, Maggie or the cat had been there – and Maggie had been out when Rebecca had visited Miss Graves and said that she'd got no sense of dark magic.

'You fell into my trap,' Maggie said, her eyes glowing with power. 'I knew the spying would work on you in the end, that you'd get angry, and that when you felt Regulus rising in the sky you'd follow the cat. Now you're here, alone . . .' She smiled and started to walk across the clearing. 'With me.'

Panic slammed into Lucy. She scrambled to her feet. 'No! Stay away!' Glancing upwards, she caught the stars of Leo in her mind. 'Shield be with me!' she cried.

Power flooded into her. Usually she lifted her hands and directed it at an object but now she grabbed on to it. She'd never tried to protect herself before and she didn't even know if it would work. A warmth started spreading over her skin. Her hopes leapt.

Maggie stopped. 'So, a shield of protection around yourself,' she said and Lucy thought she saw a gleam of respect in her eyes. 'That's quick thinking, Lucy.'

'You can't hurt me!' Lucy cried, trying to sound braver than she felt. 'Go away! I'm protected by the cloak of Leo now!'

Maggie laughed. 'Do you really think your little shield can stop me? I could destroy it in a second. I have more power than you could ever dream of.' She paused, her eyes narrowing. 'Or maybe not. I've been watching you, Lucy. Your power is quite astonishing for one your age. Maybe you do dream of power.' Her voice dropped. 'Perhaps you *are* like me.'

'I'm not!' Lucy exclaimed. 'You're a dark spirit. You're evil. I'm . . . I'm . . .'

'Good?' Maggie said, turning the word into a question. 'Is it good to use your power to control a friend, then?'

Lucy felt the blood rush to her cheeks. Maggie, in her cat form, must have been spying on her when she had stopped Faye using magic. She swallowed. 'I'm not like you,' she repeated, but even she could tell her voice didn't sound so certain.

Maggie's eyes bored into her. 'So you've never dreamed of having all the power of all the stars flowing into you? Not just Regulus, but the power of the other stars too?'

Lucy felt a flash of guilt.

'Imagine it, Lucy,' Maggie whispered temptingly. 'Imagine having the power of all nature at your fingertips. The strength of the earth, the swiftness of the wind, the coolness of water and the heat of fire. Think how that would feel.' She lowered her face closer to Lucy. 'Tell me that's not what you want.'

For a moment Lucy let herself imagine what it would be like but then she tore her thoughts away. 'No,' she exclaimed, shaking her head. 'No, I don't want that.'

Maggie looked at her and laughed. 'Then you're a fool.'

Lucy raised her hands. 'Fire be with me!' she shouted, sending a ball of fire racing at Maggie's head.

With the flick of a finger, Maggie effortlessly turned it round in mid-air. Almost before Lucy knew what was happening it was heading straight back at her. She jumped out of the way but not quite quickly enough. It grazed against her arm, burning her.

'Ow!' she cried out, looking down at the long red mark on her arm.

'You can't hurt me, Lucy,' Maggie said in an almost pitying voice.

Reaching into her pocket she pulled out a glass orb. Lucy gasped. It was the same orb she and Allegra had seen in Miss Graves's house. The golden dust danced in it as Maggie held it up. 'In this orb I hold stardust from all four Royal Stars – Summer, Autumn, Winter and Spring,' Maggie told her. 'While that power is mine, no stardust magic can harm me.'

Lucy stared at the orb. The stardust inside had once belonged to other stardust spirits. Fear trickled through her as Maggie started to come towards her, the orb held in her hand.

She tried to back away but Maggie kept approaching. 'There is no escape,' she whispered. 'Your stardust – and your power – will be mine.'

Lucy stopped as her back bumped into a tree trunk. What was she going to do now?

There was a whooshing sound in the air and Allegra, Ella and Faye flew into the clearing.

'Lucy!' Allegra gasped, stopping dead as she took in the scene in front of her.

Maggie swung round.

'Help!' Lucy cried. 'It's Maggie who's the dark spirit, not Miss Graves!'

Her friends didn't waste time on being shocked. Seeing the danger Lucy was in, they acted instantly. Allegra shot a wind straight at Maggie's feet. Faye conjured a rain cloud and Ella made a bramble bush grow between Maggie and Lucy.

Momentarily distracted, Maggie stumbled backwards. Seeing her chance, Lucy shot up into the sky.

'No,' Maggie shouted. 'There is no escape!' She cleared the wind, rain and brambles with a single click of her fingers and raised her hands. 'I'll get you! All of you. And then *all* your stardust will be mine!'

Lucy shot three balls of fire into the air. After her last attempt, she knew there was no point trying to hit Maggie with them but maybe some of the adult stardust spirits would see and come and help them. At almost the same moment Maggie flung a bolt of wind at them.

'Watch out!' Ella cried.

They scattered. The wind whistled through where they had just been flying and hit a tree, sending a shower of leaves flying into the air.

Lucy gasped as Maggie sent another bolt straight at Ella. Just in time, Ella ducked. Faye cried out as a third bolt

struck her wing. She twirled round in
the air and Allegra grabbed her.

Panic gripped Lucy. They were all
going to be killed! She shot upwards
as another bolt came searing through
the air. Suddenly she saw Regulus
above her, shining out bright and
strong.

As she felt the magic in its light, her
mind seemed to clear. Of course! *On
their own neither she nor the others could
do anything – but maybe if they used their
powers together* . . .

'Quick!' she shouted, an idea coming
to her. 'We've got to be a team!
Camouflage yourselves! Come here!'

A flash of understanding crossed her
friends' faces. In an instant they all
disappeared against the night sky. Lucy

felt the air beside her move as they
flew up to her.

Maggie frowned, rage flashing
through her eyes. 'You cannot escape
from me by camouflaging yourselves! I
can cast a spell to see through any
disguise.' She lifted her hands.

'Fire be with me!' Lucy shouted,
aiming not at Maggie but at the orb
that was still clutched in her fingers. A
ball of fire hit the orb full on,
exploding in a shower of sparks. The
orb glowed red-hot. Maggie gasped in
surprise and dropped it.

Yes! Lucy thought in delight, but the
orb landed safely, unharmed.

Maggie clicked her fingers and the
heat left the ball. Laughing, she picked
it up. 'Oh, Lucy. You really do have a

lot to learn. Did you think my precious
orb could be broken by being
dropped?'

'Thoughts be with me!' Lucy heard
Allegra mutter. Lucy caught her breath.
Was Allegra was trying to read
Maggie's thoughts?

'Try what you like, you cannot break
it,' Maggie said triumphantly. 'The
stardust from the four Royal Stars
protects my orb. Neither earth, air, fire
nor water can harm it!'

'Maybe one of them can't. But what
about all four?' Allegra gasped. She
materialized. 'We need to use our
magic together,' she hissed. 'Fire, ice, air
and earth. Quick! If we can break the
orb we'll destroy her power.'

She shot a strong gust of wind at the

orb in Maggie's hand. The orb was tossed high in the air.

Maggie exclaimed, more in annoyance than alarm, 'Aren't you listening? I've told you. You *can't* break it.'

'We'll see about that,' Allegra said. 'Lucy! Make it hot – as hot as you can!'

In a flash, Lucy understood what Allegra was trying to do. They knew each other so well; it was almost as though she could read Allegra's thoughts. 'Fire be with me!' she said, flinging a burning fireball at the orb. As they collided, sparks flew into the dark sky and the glass of the orb glowed red-hot.

'Faye!' Allegra exclaimed.

The next second a small grey hail cloud had appeared under the burning orb. As the orb plunged into the cloud and hit the freezing air, a sharp cracking noise echoed round the clearing.

'No!' Maggie gasped.

As the orb plummeted out of the cloud, Lucy could see that its smooth surface was covered with a web of tiny cracks.

Maggie raised her hands. Lucy instantly shot several fireballs at her. Distracted, Maggie swung round to fling them back. Lucy ducked and grabbed Allegra, pulling her out of the way.

'The glass is weakened,' Allegra shouted, as the orb plunged towards the earth. 'We can break it. It just needs to hit something hard. Ella! Faye!'

Ella and Faye spoke at the same time. 'Plants clear!' Ella shouted.

'Water freeze!' Faye yelled, pointing at the damp forest floor.

The undergrowth on the forest floor beneath the ball disappeared, leaving bare soil which, a second later, became rock-hard as the water in it froze solid. The ball thundered downwards.

And then suddenly it stopped.

Maggie was staring at the ball, an intense look of concentration on her face.

The ball was quivering in mid-air.

She's holding it there, Lucy thought. She knew if she could just break Maggie's concentration then the orb would fall. She raised her hands to conjure a fireball.

You could join me, Lucy.

Lucy gasped. It was Maggie's voice, but Maggie was still looking at the orb, her hand shaking in concentration as she held it in mid-air. However, her voice echoed in Lucy's head.

Together we could be strong. You have more power than I've ever seen before. I could teach you how to use it. I could show you the way . . .

An image swam into Lucy's mind. She saw herself standing in a clearing, power crackling in the air around her as she drew on the magic from all the four Royal Stars. She could almost feel the magic surging through her . . .

Your friends don't understand, Maggie's

voice went on, low and tempting. *They have no idea what it feels like to be you; to have so much power. They'll stop you using it. You need me, so join with me.*

No, Lucy thought but her answer was weak.

'Lucy?' Allegra's voice seemed to be coming from far away but, at the sound of it, the image in Lucy's mind vanished. Suddenly, instead of seeing herself surrounded by power she saw her friends and the other stardust spirits looking at her in dismay. She saw them turn their backs. She saw them walk away.

No! This time the word came from the depths of her being.

Her eyes blinked open. 'No way!' she shouted, her voice strong and clear.

'That's *not* what I want. I'm not like you, Maggie. You've got it wrong!' Anger raced through her and, pointing at Maggie, she sent another ball of fire flying straight at her heart.

Maggie cried out, breaking her concentration to deflect the fireball. Freed from her magic, the orb fell like a stone. With a crash, it smacked into the frozen ground and exploded into a thousand tiny pieces.

'My power!' Maggie shrieked as golden stardust spiralled upwards into the sky. 'My stardust!'

Before their eyes, she began to change. Grey began to streak through her dark hair, her face wrinkled, her straight back began to bend until she was hunched over, her claw-like hands

grasping uselessly at the sky. 'My
stardust,' she said, staring at Lucy, who
flew down to the ground to face her.
'You've stolen my stardust!'

'No,' Lucy said. 'It was never yours
for me to steal. You took it from other
stardust spirits.' She felt strangely calm
and in control. She knew Maggie
couldn't hurt her now.

'We could have done so much
together,' Maggie whispered. 'You
should have said yes.'

Lucy shook her head. 'I shouldn't.'
She could still see the image of the
other stardust spirits turning away from
her in her mind. She didn't want power
if it meant losing her friends.

'You'll never keep me here,' Maggie
hissed, backing off.

'Why should we want to?' Lucy said. 'You're no threat to anyone now.'

As the truth of her words hit Maggie, the dark spirit's face crumpled and her whole body seemed to sag in defeat. 'My power,' she moaned, and, turning, she half-ran into the trees.

Allegra, Ella and Faye landed beside Lucy. 'Do you think we should go after her?' Ella said, looking worried.

'No,' said Lucy. 'The adults can find her if they want.' She sat down on the ground, feeling suddenly shaky. Her shoulder was aching from where the branch had hit her and the burn on her arm throbbed. *We just defeated a dark spirit*, she thought. *Why aren't I feeling happy?* But she just felt empty and drained.

The others clearly didn't feel the same. Allegra's eyes were glowing with excitement. 'Oh wow! I can't believe we managed to break the orb!'

'We defeated a dark spirit,' Faye exclaimed. 'Just us!'

'Wasn't it amazing,' Ella put in, 'you know, when we were trying to destroy the ball? It was like our minds were all connected or something. It was so cool working together like that.'

Allegra and Faye nodded.

Faye noticed Lucy wasn't joining in. 'Lucy? Are you OK? Shall I heal the burn on your arm?'

Lucy nodded. Faye placed one hand above the wound. 'Healing be with me,' she whispered.

Lucy felt the heat leave the damaged

skin. 'Thanks,' she said as the wound faded before her eyes. 'Could you do my shoulder as well? It got hit by a branch.'

Faye nodded. When Lucy's shoulder was healed, she looked at her. 'Better?'

'Yes,' Lucy said, standing up. But she still felt odd inside.

Just then there was a swishing noise above them and Xanthe, Rebecca, Tom and Adam came flying into the clearing.

'What's been happening? We saw three fireballs in the air,' Xanthe said anxiously. 'Are you all right?'

Allegra grinned. 'We're more than all right. Wait till you hear what we've just done!'

Eleven

The adults listened in amazement as Allegra told them everything.

'This calls for a celebration,' Xanthe exclaimed. 'I think we should organize a feast.'

Rebecca nodded. 'It's not every day a dark spirit gets defeated.'

'Should we go after Maggie?' Tom said.

'No,' Xanthe replied. 'Her power will have gone. No doubt she will flee from here and never come back. Let's return to the clearing and tell the others what's been happening.' As they flew through the air, Xanthe looked at Lucy and the others very proudly. 'You did an amazing thing, girls. Four adult stardust spirits in full control of their powers would have found it hard to defeat a dark spirit.'

'We did it by working together,' Allegra said.

Ella and Faye grinned happily but Lucy still found it hard to smile. She really wanted to be happy but gradually the awareness of what she had done was creeping into her brain. She could have got herself and the

others killed by heading off after Meg
like that. If anything had happened to
them it would have been all her fault.
She should have done what Allegra said
and gone to get the adults. Why hadn't
she? Why had she insisted on going on
her own?

Because I felt strong and powerful, she
thought. *Because I felt I could do
anything.*

She shivered. If the others hadn't
arrived when they did, Maggie would
have taken her stardust. *I was so dumb*,
she thought.

Suddenly feeling that someone was
watching her, she glanced around.
Xanthe was looking at her with a
quizzical expression in her eyes. Hoping
Xanthe hadn't been reading her

thoughts, Lucy gave her a quick, awkward smile and flew on.

The other stardust spirits were amazed to hear what had been happening and soon preparations for a stardust feast were underway. As everyone bustled about, decorating the clearing with garlands of leaves, putting out tables made of giant logs, and flying home to fetch food from their houses, Lucy stayed by herself.

Xanthe came over to her. 'Are you OK?' she asked.

'I'm fine,' Lucy replied.

Xanthe squeezed her arm. 'You and the others have done so much since you first became stardust spirits. You

really should be proud of what you
have achieved today.'

Lucy swallowed, and then she
couldn't hold the words in any longer.
'No, I shouldn't. I should never have
gone after the cat. If anything had
happened to the others it would have

been all my fault.' She bit her lip. 'They tried to stop me but I wouldn't listen.'

Xanthe sighed. 'Oh, Lucy. It's true you shouldn't have gone, but there's no point in regretting it now. Just learn from what happened and be careful in the future. Don't ever get so blinded by power that you forget to listen to your friends.' She scanned Lucy's face. 'Is that *all* that's bothering you, though?'

Lucy hesitated. There was something else on her mind, but it was something she felt so ashamed of that she could hardly even bear to think about it. She looked into Xanthe's understanding blue eyes and the truth came out. 'Maggie said I was like her,' she whispered huskily. 'She said I wanted power. She asked me to join her and I . . .' She swallowed but made herself tell Xanthe the truth. 'I almost wanted to.'

'Almost,' Xanthe said softly. 'But not quite. And that is what makes you different from Maggie. You chose your friends over power.' She squeezed Lucy's shoulders. 'There's a thin line between good and evil, Lucy, and with the amount of power you have, it's a line you're going to have to walk all your life. It won't be easy.' She paused and her voice lowered. 'Believe me, I know.'

And suddenly Lucy realized that Xanthe did. She saw the power shining out of Xanthe's eyes, as much power, maybe, as she'd seen in Maggie's. Lucy blinked and felt a weight roll off her shoulders. It wasn't just her. Xanthe had had to make the same choices as she herself faced and she'd chosen what was right. *If she can do it, then I can too,* Lucy thought determinedly. A relieved sigh escaped her.

'Having power is wonderful,' Xanthe said, her voice full of understanding, 'but not if it just makes you want more power, and not if it costs you your friends. Friends are so important, Lucy. Not just because friendship is precious but also because when people work as a team they're stronger than any one person can be on their own. It's not only that they have different magic powers, but they have different minds too and different strengths. Four people working together, as you, Allegra, Ella and Faye did today, will always be more powerful than one. Remember that.'

Lucy nodded. She knew she would. 'Thanks.' She shook her head. 'I can't believe it was Maggie who was the dark spirit.' A thought crossed her mind. 'What will happen to all the stardust that she kept in the orb? Will it just go back to the stars?'

'No,' replied Xanthe. 'Now it has been released it will return to the people it was stolen from.'

Lucy frowned. 'Miss Graves used to keep asking for her dust. Could she have been talking about stardust? She might have been one of the stardust spirits that Maggie stole stardust from.'

Xanthe looked thoughtful. 'Maybe. I should probably go and find out. Would you like to come with me?'

'Yes please,' Lucy said.

When Allegra heard that they were going to Miss Graves's house she wanted to come too and so the three of them set off through the trees. When they reached Lavender Cottage, Lucy saw no sign of Maggie's things. It looked like Maggie had definitely left.

For good, Lucy thought in relief, remembering Xanthe's words.

They flew up to the bedroom windows. The first two bedrooms were empty but the third room had a slightly open window and looking through it they saw Miss Graves lying in bed.

'Is she OK?' Allegra whispered to Xanthe.

'Yes,' Xanthe said slowly, her eyes on Miss Graves. 'She's fine. She's just asleep.'

As she spoke, Miss Graves's eyelids fluttered.

Lucy was about to camouflage herself but to her surprise, Xanthe stopped her. 'No. Don't camouflage yourself,' she said, her gaze never leaving the old lady's face.

Miss Graves's eyes opened. She looked at the window. 'People flying,' she said, sounding confused. 'People flying outside.' She rubbed a hand across her face. 'I must be dreaming.' She blinked and then suddenly looked as if she'd remembered something. She stared at them. 'No, no, I'm not dreaming,' she said in a stronger voice. 'You're stardust spirits.'

A smile broke out on Xanthe's face. 'Yes,' she said, opening the window by magic and flying inside. Lucy and Allegra exchanged looks and followed her. Miss Graves looked at them in wonderment.

'Do you remember now?' Xanthe said.

Miss Graves nodded. 'I do. I was a stardust spirit but then,' she shivered and a look of alarm crossed her face, 'Maggie came along.' She spoke the name with dread.

'Tell us what happened,' Xanthe said gently.

Miss Graves rubbed her forehead.

'My memory's a bit confused. I remember breaking my ankle a few years ago and needing someone to care for me. Maggie applied for the job. She seemed very nice at first but then . . .' she shook her head as if remembering was too painful, 'then . . . then she took my stardust. I can't remember much since then. I remember moving from house to house and feeling weaker and weaker every day – getting more and more confused.'

'That was part of Maggie's magic,' Xanthe said gravely. 'She must have cast a spell on you to make you forget about being a stardust spirit. Looking after you would have been the perfect excuse for her. She could come and go as she pleased and move you to a new place to find new stardust spirits to trap, and you wouldn't complain because you were under her spell.'

'I did forget about being a stardust spirit. I felt that I had lost something,' Miss Graves said. 'But I remember now.'

Lucy suddenly realized that although Miss Graves was still an old lady, her eyes, once faded, now looked bright, her skin seemed less wrinkled and she was sitting up straighter.

'I remember dancing with the stars,' Miss Graves said dreamily, as if seeing images in her mind. 'I remember feeling the wind in my hair, my friends around me. I remember working in the woods and doing magic.' She broke off and looked at Xanthe. Her voice suddenly trembled. 'Will I ever be able to turn into a stardust spirit again?' she asked.

Lucy held her breath and waited for Xanthe's answer.

Xanthe took Miss Graves's hand and smiled. 'If you believe in stardust,' she said softly.

'Oh, I believe in stardust,' Miss Graves said. She pushed back the bed covers and stood up. 'I believe in stardust.' She looked at them all and then out of the window. *'I believe in stardust!'*

As the last word left her lips, Miss Graves's body seemed to dissolve into sparkling light and the next second she was flying in the air. Her grey hair escaped from its bun, and a green dress, the mark of a spring spirit, swirled around her.

A look of pure delight lit up her face. 'I'm a stardust spirit again!'

Xanthe flew up and took her hand. 'Come with us. Fly with us.'

Miss Graves smiled. 'I will.'

And with that, the four of them flew out of the window and left Lavender Cottage behind. Over the fields they flew, and into the woods.

Lucy glanced across at Allegra. Her eyes were sparkling and she smiled happily at Lucy.

As they reached the clearing, Lucy saw that it was ready for the celebration to begin. The tables were piled high with food, garlands of red, gold and orange leaves decorated the clearing, and a thousand fireflies lit up the clearing like tiny stars of light. Ella and Faye were helping to set out the last of the food and as they saw Miss Graves they stared and then waved excitedly. Allegra swooped down to join them, an explanation already spilling out of her mouth. Xanthe and Miss Graves followed.

However, Lucy hung back. Just for a moment she wanted to see the clearing from a distance.

She flew to sit in a fork in the aspen tree. The very tree she'd been sitting under when she'd first discovered she could stop objects in mid-air. Above her the remaining aspen leaves trembled as they clung to the branches. Far above them Regulus shone out. Looking around at the clearing, Lucy felt its magic spark over her skin and a feeling of intense happiness spread through her. She didn't want all the magic of the four Royal Stars. She didn't want to be powerful and on her own. She didn't want anything but to be a summer spirit having fun with her friends.

Below her she saw Allegra, Ella and Faye starting to chase each other around the clearing.

Xanthe's right, she thought. *We have done so much since we first became stardust spirits, we really have.*

Her friends waved.

'Come on, Luce,' Allegra called up to her. 'We're playing tick!'

'Coming!' Lucy called. She smiled. *I wonder what will happen to us next?* she thought.

The aspen leaves trembled. 'More, much more,' they whispered as she flew away.

Do you love magic, unicorns and fairies?

Join the sparkling

Linda Chapman

fan club today!

It's FREE!

You will receive a sparkle pack, including:

Stickers   **Badge**

Membership card   **Glittery pencil**

Plus four Linda Chapman newsletters every year,
packed full of fun, games, news and competitions.
And look out for a special card on your birthday!

How to join:

Visit lindachapman.co.uk and enter your details

Send your name, address, date of birth* and email address (if you have one) to:
**Linda Chapman Fan Club, Puffin Marketing,
80 Strand, London, WC2R 0RL**